Modern Curriculum Press

BEGINNING
TO
READ
Series

ARA'S Amazing SPINNING WHEEL

by
David R. Collins

illustrated by Val Mayerik

Softcover edition published simultaneously in Canada by Globe/Modern Curriculum Press, Toronto.

Library of Congress Cataloging-in-Publication Data

Collins, David R.
  Ara's amazing spinning wheel.

  Summary: Ara, a male orb spider, hatches out of his egg, grows to maturity, spins his own web, finds a mate, and has the satisfaction of seeing his own baby spiders hatch.
  1. Spiders—Juvenile fiction. [1. Spiders—Fiction]
I. Meyerik, Val, ill. II. Title.
PZ10.3.C689Ar 1987   [Fic]   87-11144
ISBN 0-8136-5181-6
ISBN 0-8136-5681-8 (pbk.)

1 2 3 4 5 6 7 8 9   87 88 89 90

MODERN CURRICULUM PRESS

A Division of Simon & Schuster
13900 Prospect Road, Cleveland, Ohio 44136

This is a cocoon.
It is a little ball of silk.
It hangs from the leaf of a tree.
Nothing moves on the outside of the
   cocoon.
But something is moving inside.
Hundreds of tiny eggs are opening.
Baby spiders are being born.

Ara is an orb spider.
Slowly he opens his eight eyes.
Slowly he stretches his eight legs.
He breathes.
He breaks out of his egg.
Something kicks Ara in the side.
It is another baby spider.
Ara is kicked in the head.
He is surrounded by other baby spiders.

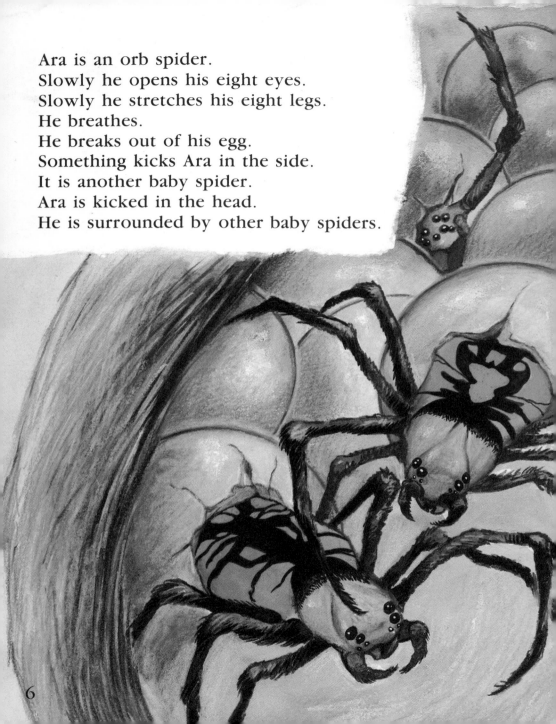

It is dark inside the cocoon.
It is crowded.
The baby spiders want to get out.
Ara kicks at the walls of the cocoon.
The other baby spiders kick too.
The cocoon rips open.

Ara has a spinning wheel inside his
   stomach.
This spinning wheel spins liquid silk
   threads.
The threads harden when they come
   out of Ara's stomach.
Ara watches some of his brothers and
   sisters.
They use their spinning wheels.
They release long silk threads.
The baby spiders lower themselves to
   the ground on their threads.

8

Ara spins a long thread.
Along comes a breeze.
Whoosh!
The wind carries off a handful of spiders.
Ara goes with them.
They sail in the air like tiny balloons.
Ara dips and glides in the breeze.
One orb spider catches onto a tree branch.
Another lands on a church steeple.
The wind carries Ara upward and
    onward.

Ara looks higher.
A crow swoops and attacks the sailing
    spiders.
Suddenly the breeze stops.
Ara drifts downward.
Ara lands on a big soft leaf.
It is part of a spreading lilac bush.
Ara watches one of his brothers drift to
    a rock below.

Nearby the grass moves.
A lizard appears on the rock.
Quickly the lizard's tongue strikes out.
The tiny spider cannot get away.

Ara looks around.
His legs feel the branch he is on.
It is a strong branch.
There are many branches close by.
Orb spiders like to build their homes
    among strong branches.

Again Ara puts his spinning wheel to work.
Silk threads slip out of the openings on
    Ara's stomach.
The openings are called spinnerets.
Ara drops to the branch below.
Then he swings to another branch.
Back and forth he jumps.
Up and down he climbs.
The silk threads cross and harden in the air.
They become a sturdy web.

13

By nightfall Ara has finished.
His new home is a fine lace circle.
It swings lazily in the moonlight.
Ara sits in the middle of his web.
Soon he drifts off to sleep.

14

Suddenly Ara wakes up.
Bright rays of the sun stream through
    the lilac bush.
But it is not the light that has awakened Ara.
Something is shaking the web.
Ara strains to see.
Orb spiders do not have good eyesight.
But Ara can see in his web.
Step by step a wasp moves closer.
Wasps love to eat spiders.

15

Ara works fast.
He leaps to the side and runs around
    the wasp.
Ara shoots out silk threads.
He jumps back and forth around the
    wasp.
The wasp cannot move as fast as Ara.
Quickly he wraps the wasp in silk
    threads.
But the wasp is big.
He struggles and rips many of the
    threads away.
Yet Ara is too quick for him.
The orb spider leaps to the right, then
    the left.
The spinning wheel pours out the
    threads.

The wasp still struggles.
His open mouth tries to bite Ara.
Quickly Ara slips behind his attacker.
He bites the wasp with tiny fangs.
Soon the wasp is dead.
The poison in Ara's fangs has done its
    job.

Ara has no teeth to eat the wasp.
But orb spiders have special juices.
They can turn the wasp tissue into
    liquid.
Ara sucks the liquid tissue out of the
    wasp.
Then he wraps the wasp in more silk
    threads.
The wasp will make many more meals
    for Ara.

Morning dew covers the lilac bush each
    day.
Ara drinks the fresh cool drops.
His web catches more bugs and flies to
    eat.
The days slip into weeks, then months.

One morning Ara lies resting.
His web begins to toss from side to
    side.
Ara holds tight to the silk threads.
He opens his eyes wide.
A boy is picking lilacs close by.
Again the spider web shakes.
Ara sits still.
Orb spiders do not attack human
    beings.

Soon the boy has a handful of flowers.
He walks away from the bush.
The boy did not even see Ara.
The spider's brown and green color
    helped to hide him.

The sound of hooting owls fills the
    summer nights.
The moon shines on the web in the
    bush.
The silk threads gleam.
They swing lightly in the wind.

But one night the moon does not shine.
It hides behind dark clouds.
White streaks flash across the sky.
Thunder rolls and rumbles.
Giant raindrops fall.
Ara races along the silk threads of his
    home.
The rain and wind rip holes in the web.
Quickly Ara puts his spinning wheel to
    work.

The storm grows wilder.
Suddenly a twig flies through the air.
It knocks Ara to the ground below.
Ara lies in the wet grass.
Slowly he tries to get up.
He stumbles and falls.
One of his eight legs is gone.
It was broken off by the twig.
For a long time Ara lies on the ground.
Then he goes to sleep.

When Ara wakes, his skin feels old and
    tight.
He wiggles and jerks back and forth.
He pulls and tugs.
Hours become days as Ara squirms.
He does not eat.
All he does is pull off his old skin.
Finally, the job is done.
Ara wears a new skin.
He has grown out of his old skin into a
    new skin.
This is called molting.
He has even grown a new leg!

Carefully Ara begins to rebuild his
home.
The spinning wheel is working fine.
Back and forth he runs on the bush.
Fine silk threads appear once more.
By nightfall Ara has a new home.

Ara has a web of strong silk thread.
He has plenty to eat.
He enjoys the sun, the wind and the
    moon.
But something is missing.
What could it be?

Early the next morning Ara leaves his
    web.
He is looking for a mate.
Surely somewhere there is a female orb
    spider without a mate.
Ara swings from branch to branch on
    the bush.
Suddenly Ara stops.
A female orb spider sits alone in her
    fine web.

Ara steps lightly onto a silk thread of
her web.
Gently he shakes the thread.
It is his way of knocking on the female
spider's door.
Like Ara, her eyes are not too good.
But her legs feel the movement.
She knows she has a visitor.
Slowly Ara steps forward.
The female spider is much bigger than
he is.
She could eat him if she wished.

Ara is lucky.

The female spider has been waiting for a mate.

She welcomes Ara into her web home.

Together Ara and his mate add new silk threads to their home.

It swings lightly in the wind.

Together they share the days and nights.

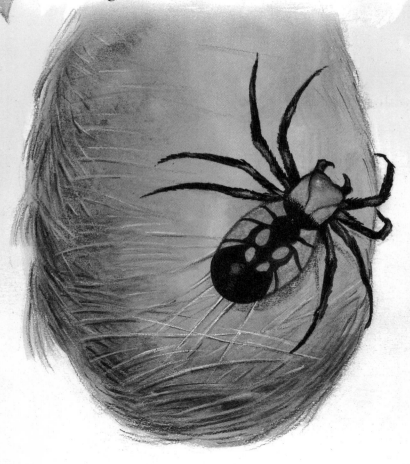

One day Ara's mate begins to spin a
small ball of silk.
It is a cocoon.
Ara watches his mate fill the cocoon
with eggs.
It is twilight.
Many days later, Ara sits in his web and
watches the cocoon.
Nothing moves on the outside of the
cocoon.
But something is moving inside.
Baby spiders are ready to be born.

Ara watches.

Small holes appear in the cocoon.

Some spiders drop to the ground on silk
threads.

Other baby spiders are swept away on
the wind.

New spinning wheels are at work again.

But Ara's spinning wheel has done its
job.

Slowly Ara closes his eyes, and sleeps.